The Palace

PRAISE FOR *STORYSHARES*

"One of the brightest innovators and game-changers in the education industry."
– Forbes

"Your success in applying research-validated practices to promote literacy serves as a valuable model for other organizations seeking to create evidence-based literacy programs."
- Library of Congress

"We need powerful social and educational innovation, and Storyshares is breaking new ground. The organization addresses critical problems facing our students and teachers. I am excited about the strategies it brings to the collective work of making sure every student has an equal chance in life."
– Teach For America

"Around the world, this is one of the up-and-coming trailblazers changing the landscape of literacy and education."
- International Literacy Association

"It's the perfect idea. There's really nothing like this. I mean wow, this will be a wonderful experience for young people."   - Andrea Davis Pinkney, Executive Director, Scholastic

"Reading for meaning opens opportunities for a lifetime of learning. Providing emerging readers with engaging texts that are designed to offer both challenges and support for each individual will improve their lives for years to come. Storyshares is a wonderful start."
- David Rose, Co-founder of CAST & UDL

The Palace

Sophie Rathmann

STORYSHARES

Story Share, Inc.
New York. Boston. Philadelphia.

Storyshares
Story Share, Inc.
24 N. Bryn Mawr Avenue #340
Bryn Mawr, PA 19010-3304
www.storyshares.org

Inspiring reading with a new kind of book.

Interest Level: High School
Grade Level Equivalent: 3.4

9781642612004

Book design by Storyshares

Printed in the United States of America

Storyshares Presents

1

The Palace has loomed high on the hill for as long as the people can remember. It seems older than time, eternally in shadows. It is known as The Palace and nothing else. No one lives there. No one dares push back the gates. Everything gets quieter near The Palace. It's as if the shadows have a physical weight, and a fog fills the ears of listeners and softens the footfalls of those who dare to walk the streets.

The Palace is old and sad. The people fear it. They have good reason. For as long as they can remember, it has always happened on the seventh day of the seventh month. Someone is chosen to push past the gates. Someone leaves, and they never return. It is something the people do not speak of, something they try to forget. But The Palace is at the center of town. They cannot escape it.

When their children begin to ask why, the people simply explain that this is the way it has always been. They fear what would happen if they failed to send someone to The Palace. They fear the shadow that they can sense within its walls. So, every year, without fail, their feet shuffle through the crooked, cobbled streets to a gathering where no one looks anyone else in the eyes. Lots are drawn, quiet tears are shed, and one person enters The Palace.

It is the same this year, the people think. They shuffle through the streets with their heads down and their hearts in their throats. It is almost dark. They flow into the square like a tide of shadows. Each one has brought a candle, unlit.

A circle forms wordlessly. Then the bag is brought forth—ominous, heavy. All that can be heard is the clacking of the stones within the velvet prison. Slowly, the drawstrings are opened, and one shaking hand reaches inside. The whole circle holds its breath, some in hope of good, others secretly wishing the worst.

A black stone emerges, clutched firmly in stout fingers. They are safe. The bag changes hands, and one by one, black stones are drawn. Those who have drawn them hide their joy for the sake of the others, who watch with mounting fear. It goes on and on, over and over, a cycle within a cycle. Unbroken. And then, finally, white.

The white stone emerges, clutched firmly in the young, pale hands of a beautiful girl. The villagers know her, not well, but they know her. She sings in the evenings with a voice made of light. They will miss her.

The Palace

2

Her deep blue eyes stay strong, framed by long hair the color of burnished bronze. She curls the white stone into her fist and holds out the bag. The villagers who have drawn their stones slowly shuffle towards her, dropping them one by one back into place. There is relief and loss in the air, mourning and selfish joy.

As the last stone is placed back in the bag, her parents light their candles. From those candles, the rest are lit, all except one. The girl places her own candle back in her pocket, unlit. She is no longer one of them. She is alone, and yet, this parade of lights will walk her to the gates.

They surround her silently, in a last sign of hope, of solitude, of love. Silently, they wind their way up the hill. Past the faces of children stuck in the windows—those who are too young to understand what is going on. All they see is a parade of candles. They do not see the girl who holds a stone.

A chill rushes through the night, and the candles sputter when at last they reach the tall black gates. On this night, they are unlocked. No one knows who holds the key. The gates are locked on all other nights.

Slowly, a ring of people forms around the girl. She has not shed any tears, not yet, which is strange. She is braver than they knew. Now it is time for her to go. She hands the bag to her father and the white stone to her mother. Her parents have shed their tears. The girl wipes them away. There are a few softly whispered words, and then she turns to the gates.

Her head is held high. Her cheeks are dry. If she is afraid, her eyes do not show it. She lays a hand on the old iron gates and pushes. They open slowly on hinges that shriek from a year of disuse. She steps inside, and the gates clang shut behind her.

The Palace

3

One by one, the little lights behind her make their way back to their homes, until there are only two left. The girl takes care not to look back at them as she walks onward, past the wall and the gates, to the black door that seems to gape like a mouth even when closed. As she steps inside, the last two lights go out.

Her name is Laurel. Her name is Laurel, and this is her world now. She cannot go back. She cannot escape. She must go through for as long and as far as she can. Who knows what will happen after that? If The Palace knows, it certainly won't tell.

She is alone in a dark and silent world, and it is strange to her, but she holds her head high and steps away from the door. She has no goal in mind, so she moves aimlessly. A white figure in a world of shadow, floating from room to room.

She never finds food in The Palace, but she is never hungry. She never finds water in The Palace, but she is never thirsty. She never finds light in The Palace but finds that she does not need it.

As she passes through a room, her mind wanders. She imagines what it might look like: a rich, expansive ballroom—but no. No, she can feel an ornate table beneath her fingertips. Her fingers are her guides in this world of shadow. They flutter over walls, tapestries, and gilded candelabras.

In the beginning, she is clumsy and slow, knocking into chairs and tables and walls. She moves more cautiously. She learns, and she does not realize it, but she begins to move like a shadow, herself. Her wanderings go from nervously excited to mundane. She grows used to the landscape. She grows bored. That's when it happens.

4

She is standing, alone, in the center of a room she has never been in before. The air is still. She is still. Something else moves. She hears the skittering of movement directly ahead of her, and for the first time, she is truly frightened. She is not alone. She is no longer alone. Was she ever alone?

She takes a silent step backward. The thing scuttles closer. She stops. It hisses. Then she turns and runs, and it spits and chases after her. Her heart is pounding, pounding in her ears. She flees back the way she came, back into the halls she knows, but she can't escape it. It does not stop.

Her breath is fast and shallow. Her mind is white with fear. Then she remembers the candle in her pocket. It is the only thing she has left from that outside world. Perhaps, if she lights it . . .

She dashes to the left, down a staircase. She knows where to run now. Faster, faster. It follows. At long last, her feet skitter into the room she needs. Blind, she lets her fingers find the matches by instinct. They do not fail her. Slowly, she backs away into a corner and waits.

The thing is in the room with her. She can feel it. Then, from her left, she hears it. A scratch of claws on the stone floor. She lights the match and cries out in pain at the flash of light. Light is something she has not seen in a long time. The creature shrieks and dashes away, and Laurel drops the match. It goes out. She is glad.

It takes ages for the afterimage to burn its way out of her eyes. She is surprised. The light never hurt before. Still, she carries the matches with her after that. She wanders more cautiously. She does not go back to that empty room. She does not explore many new ones, but she knows deep in her heart that that will not stop the creature.

The Palace

5

She cannot say how much time has passed when the rooms begin to grow lighter. At first, she does not believe her own eyes. She can see the tapestries and the gilded candelabras. She does not know why. That is, she does not know why until she finds a mirror.

She stares into the mirror. Her own face stares back. It takes a long time to notice what is different. Her eyes are red, red where they were once blue. She has changed. This world of shadows has changed her. Or perhaps she has changed to fit this world.

Now she knows that if or when the creature comes back, she will be ready. She will see it coming. It does not know. That is when she resolves to fight. She will not go quietly. She will not fail, as the others have so obviously. Why else does it think it can have her? It only thinks that because it has gotten everyone else.

The creature has never been beaten. She will be the one to beat it, she swears, looking into those red eyes in the mirror. She will do whatever it takes. She will change to beat the creature. She will win.

She begins exploring again, daring the monster to come out. She ignores her fear, swallows it. Like a shadow, she ghosts from room to room. Methodical and slow, watching and waiting. She grips the matches tightly and peers into the darkness. It is a long time to wait, but at last she hears it. Feels it. The creature is back.

Her heart pounds in her throat, and she stands once more alone in the center of an empty, quiet room. But this time, she can see. So, she sees as the dark, spindly beast enters the room. A chill runs down her spine. It is so far from human, so far from natural. There is no ignoring its wrongness.

And then, the unthinkable. A second beast enters the room. She is no longer ready. She is scared. Her hands shake as she removes the matches from her cloak. The creatures stop, hissing quietly. She freezes. Still. Still. Still. She remains frozen in their gaze. They remain trapped in hers. They are staring. She is staring back.

For a long moment, nothing happens. Then they leap, hissing and spitting, towards her.

The Palace

6

She lights the match, watching as they rear back from the circle of light. She moves towards them, singing her own song of defiance, dancing her own dance of hope. The creatures move away from the flame and the heat, but her eyes are different. The flames do not hurt. The shadows do not hurt. She is a creature of both.

For a moment, she is winning. Then another beast enters the room, hissing and spitting. The others, bolstered by the arrival of an ally, attack, and she flees. Back the way she has come, back towards that same room, but she knows that her matches are no longer a surprise. The three creatures, together, will not allow themselves to be overpowered by something as intangible as light.

She needs a weapon. She smiles. She is in a castle. She has more weapons than she could ever hope to use. Wrenching a spear out of its place on the wall, she turns and looks back. She can see them advancing through the shadows. She hears the clicks and hisses. Heart racing, she relights her candle and places it to the side.

The monsters slow, hiss, and continue towards her. She braces herself, balancing on the balls of her feet. She takes a deep breath and raises the spear. The first creature jumps at her with a screech, and she raises the spear blindly, flinching away from its jaws.

There is a squeal of pain from the creature, but she feels one claw rip through her white dress, biting into her shoulder like a red-hot flame. She falls backwards, the weight of the creature taking her down.

Finally, her eyes center back on the monster. She has impaled it through the stomach, but it is on top of her, writhing, still alive. With a scream of pain, anger, and sheer determination, she throws it off and drags its claws out of her body. She pulls hard on the spear and hears the wet sound of it leaving the monster's body. Then she strikes, again and again, until it lies dead at her feet in the pool of light from the candle.

She spins around looking for the other two creatures, but they are gone. The spear falls from her hand, and her eyes grow heavy. Laurel sinks into unconsciousness as a great pain spreads through her whole body. When she wakes, she becomes aware of her wounds for the first time. The monster's claws, like razor blades, have sliced past her clothing.

She curses her stupidity to think that having light would beat a monster—how silly. Of course she needs a weapon to beat them, but she also needs armor. She finally understands what she must do in order to beat them. She must become a warrior. It is that or die, and she has sworn to beat them.

Slowly, she makes her way to her feet, and she stumbles away, spear in hand. Quickly, she finds what she needs in a room she had explored long ago. As she finishes bandaging her wounds, she catches sight of herself in the mirror. This time, spotting the difference is easy. A pair of thick, black horns sits atop her head. She stares as her reflection moves, as she moves, to touch them.

They are as solid as the rest of her, like the dark crown of a victorious warrior. She smiles and watches her reflection do the same. Laurel will strike fear into the hearts of the creatures in the castle. They will know her wrath. It is far from over. In fact, it is truly the beginning.

7

She takes her time to heal, then to prepare. She gathers the weapons in her wing of the castle. She makes a pack of medical supplies. She trades her torn white dress for a grey tunic and cloak that she finds in one of the bedrooms. She trains with her weapons and slowly grows stronger. Then it is time to go further. It is time to find the armor she so desperately needed in the last fight.

She begins to journey farther out into the reaches of The Palace, into rooms she has not visited since her first reckless exploration of The Palace. Then she passes beyond. Her horns make their purpose known as she explores. They provide her with a sixth sense for danger beyond sight or getting chills. They guide her safely through halls devoid of the black, spindly, inhuman creatures.

At long last, she finds the room she is looking for. Suit after suit of armor stands solidly in the center of a long hall. Her red eyes reflect off of the pale surfaces as she inspects one after another, row after row, until she reaches the third pedestal. It stands empty.

Her heart pounds. Hope bounds in her heart. Someone else has made it here before. She wonders quickly if they are still out there, then dismisses the thought. She does not have time to worry about anyone else. She is alone.

She moves down the line, until she arrives at the seventh plinth. The armor is perfect. It is black and reflects no light. It is unused and in stellar condition. The sword in its sheath is as sharp as the day it was made and as black as the deepest of shadows. It is a weapon that fits her perfectly. It is her weapon.

After that, she doesn't go anywhere without the armor or the sword. She trains and waits and explores. Sometimes, she fights. Then she discovers why the creatures are not attacking her, why they haven't been seeking her out.

She is making her way down a new hall when her horns give her a warning. Danger is close. Her eyes flick to the right. She can see light and shadows, dancing their way down the hall. Then she hears it, the sound of a sword.

None of these things are like the creatures. She remembers the missing armor. She rounds the corner of the hall and draws her sword.

A stream of creatures surrounds a soldier in bluish-white armor. The hall around him is lit with candlelight, and so they skitter anxiously at the edges of the light, attacking one or two at a time. The soldier is fending them off with his sword, dealing well-timed blows, but he is surrounded.

Laurel lets out a scream of fury and charges at the creatures on her side of the hall. They hiss and shriek, diving towards her. She is not protected by the light. Her sword flies in circles, blocking and parrying, stabbing and cutting.

For the first time, she sees the monsters truly afraid as their angry hisses turn to shrieks of pain and defeat. The floor becomes littered with the corpses of the spindly beasts, until the last of them either lay dead at her feet or have retreated back the way they had came.

She has won this battle.

8

Slowly, she turns to the soldier in the pool of light and lowers her sword. She regrets it instantly as his own sword is raised to her throat, and she is backed into the wall.

"What are you?" The voice is sharp and deep but surprisingly young.

"I'm human!" Laurel cries out, flinching away from the sword. "I swear!"

"No, you're not." The soldier says, but he drops his sword. "No human has horns or burning red eyes. You must be a demon."

Laurel shivers. She has heard that word whispered before but only in stories. Only when the people of the village spoke about The Palace. The stories had been few and far between, but now she remembers something.

"No. That's what they are." She points at the carcasses of the beasts.

"That's what everyone says." The soldier turns away. "I don't care. Be a demon or don't." He begins to walk away.

"Wait! Don't you need help?"

"No," he replies without looking back. "I've always done fine on my own."

As he leaves, a part of Laurel seems to shrink and wither away. She is human, isn't she? *Isn't she*? But the soldier hasn't changed. He is still completely human. Why her? Why is she different?

As she turns and walks away, she understands one thing: her fight is her own. The soldier will not help her, and he does not want her help. She is still alone. So she wages her own war against the demons, seeking them out and holding true to her own promise. They will fear her. She will win. And yet, she is lonelier than ever.

When she changes next, she isn't surprised, but she no longer feels like changing is winning. Her wings are as black as the rest of her—the armor, the sword, and the horns. She wonders if she will grow claws next. Perhaps she is a demon. Perhaps this is how they are made.

Unconsciously, she begins singing wherever she goes like a caged bird. Although she has wings, she feels more trapped than ever. The Palace is one enormous cage, and she feels like a rat put there for entertainment, pitted against impossible odds.

She continues to battle her way through with a one-mindedness that begins to scare even herself. She has lost her purpose. She no longer knows what she is fighting for. For the longest time, she was fighting to not be alone. She was fighting to survive and find someone, anyone, maybe even to return to the village. Now she is not alone, but she is lonelier than ever.

She knows that she cannot go back to who she was before. She cannot go back to the village. She cannot go home. So she sings, sometimes with words, sometimes without. She sings songs she knows. She creates new ones. She remembers songs she thought were long forgotten. She sings more and battles less, until she stops fighting at all.

9

She finds a bell tower. It is empty and silent. The ropes for the bells broke long ago, so they are spread like shattered glass on the floor. She takes off her armor, lays down her sword, and flies to the top of the tower.

The windows in The Palace do not show the outside world. Instead, they show swirling shadows and things that never are. The windows of The Palace are lies. She sits and sings for a long time, and her songs are full of memories and pain, regret and wishes. She sings and bares her soul for no one to hear.

But he hears anyway, and he listens. It has been a long time since he last saw the she-demon, but who else could it be? Her voice brings back memories of what he has lost, and he stands outside the door and listens, far enough away that she does not see his light.

He pulls himself away from the tower and goes back to battle, but every night he secretly returns. He recognizes some of her songs, and the others he knows in his heart. She sings of everything he fights for, and so he remembers. He remembers how he used to hope for company. How every year, he would become eager at the thought of a new companion. How every year, his hopes fell through, until his heart grew cold.

He remembers why he began his war. He remembers the village he left behind. He realizes that she knows all of these things, too. He remembers how she fought when she came to his aid, like a fiery black whirlwind that drove fear into the very souls of the demons before her. He remembers her passion and her fury and her fear when he turned his sword against her. How she had pleaded that she was human.

He remembers turning away, leaving her behind, and never looking back. How wrong he was, he realizes. All along, she has been more human than him.

10

At long last, he enters the tower. He peers up through the broken bells and sees the she-demon. But she's not a demon, she's an angel with black wings and a human soul.

"Forgive me."

She stops singing, and her red eyes find him easily. He is standing in a pool of light, as always, carrying a lone candle. He sets it down and hoists her own sword by the blade, extending the hilt upwards, towards her.

"Forgive me. You're as human as I am—more, even."

She spreads her wings and soars down to meet him. Her eyes narrow, and she takes the sword tentatively. He tells her everything, about how he had forgotten what he was fighting for until he had stumbled upon the tower many weeks ago. How he had remembered what it was like to still have hope of finding others. He even tells her about what he remembers of the village, how he was chosen. How young and scared he was. He tells her how he's survived, what he's lost. He tells her everything.

He finishes with his name. His name is Damerin. His name is Damerin, and he's been fighting alone in this world for too long. When he asks her to fight again, this time with him, she can't say no. She joins him, and together they renew one another's hopes, dreams, and ambitions for battle.

They are fighting as much for each other as they were ever fighting for the village. They make the perfect team. He is the light to her dark. She is the fear, and he is the mercy. Together, they are unstoppable.

They forge their way through hall after hall, clearing one floor of demons and then the next. And the next and the next. There are injuries and fights, but they are two sides of the same coin, and their partnership is irrevocable.

He has been in The Palace for almost seven years. She has been in The Palace for almost three. He entered The

Palace when he was fourteen. She entered it at seventeen. This fight has hardened them. They are not who they were when they entered The Palace. They have seen enough evil for a thousand lifetimes, and they have fought against it every day.

The Palace

11

Now, the seventh day of the seventh month is approaching again. In the village, there are rumors. The Palace stands as lonely and foreboding as ever. The people fear it as they always have, but this year, something has changed.

Now it is said that if you approach The Palace on a clear, silent night, you can hear a woman singing. Some laugh at the story, while others mutter darkly. Some call it the voice of an angel, and others call it a siren. Still others call it a ghost. To some, the voice is remarkably familiar, as if they've heard it before. They shake their heads. They must be wrong.

There are only two people in the whole town who know the truth, but they dare not speak it. Their daughter's voice slips its silvery notes out of The Palace every night. They know not whether it is a ghost or a siren. Secretly, they hope that it is neither. Every night, they climb the cobbled streets on the hill until they arrive at the tall black gates, and then they listen until their daughter stops singing.

One night, another woman joins them. She lost her son to The Palace years ago. She understands what the other parents are thinking and hoping. She begins to hope with them. Slowly, the group expands. Everyone who has lost a child or a sibling, or even a friend, begins keeping the silent vigil. Most of them can't explain why, but the woman's voice gives them hope. It is the only sign of life that has ever escaped The Palace.

No one knows when it begins, but everyone who comes begins bringing unlit candles. They remain unlit, night after night, until a fortnight before the seventh day of the seventh month. Matches are slowly passed around until the small group is filled with light, listening to the soft song drifting from The Palace. That's when it happens.

As the last note of the woman's song finishes, the villagers begin to hum their own tune. Then they grow louder and louder still, until they find their own words, and they sing their hope and their grief into the sky. *Let this year be different*, they think as they sing. *Let this year be different.*

Inside The Palace, Damerin hears the singing first. He looks up, and Laurel is running to him, a smile on her face larger than any he's ever seen. He's smiling the same way. He knows, and then they are holding each other and crying and laughing. The village has not forgotten them.

The Palace

12

Their hope, their determination, and their courage is renewed. Their purpose is clearer than ever. They proceed to battle as they have never battled before. If he was light, then he now shines like the sun. If she was a dark whirlwind, she becomes an unstoppable hurricane. Together, they hunt down the last of the demons.

The monsters are larger and more terrifying than they have ever been, but the indomitable pair cannot be stopped. They are two edges of the same sword, steel forged in the same fires. On the thirteenth night, they know that their victory hangs in the balance. They are, for the first time, tired in The Palace. The dark magic is failing. They must either wipe it out or succumb to the demons and allow the darkness to return.

Laurel's horns tell her that the deepest part of the demon's domain, their last stronghold, is the tallest keep in the center of The Palace. They have rid the surrounding courtyards and towers and halls of the demons. This is their last stand. They must clear it tonight before the seventh night of the seventh month arrives. Before the dark magic here is bolstered by the arrival of a new victim.

They cross the courtyard together: one surrounded by shadow, the other by light. Their blades are drawn, held in hands that have grown firm with years of experience. They have earned every scar thus far, and they will earn more tonight. Those scars have been the price of the ground that they have gained. Those scars are the price of their victories. Tonight, they aim to win.

The moon is absent from the sky, and the stars shine like an infinity of candles as they enter the keep. Inside, the walls seem to ooze with evil, and Laurel's eyes can see the spindly, grotesque creatures on the ceiling, the walls, and the floors. They are hissing and spitting, and without hesitation, they attack.

Laurel and Damerin swing smoothly into action, blades singing and slicing. One after another, the monsters fall, hissing and shrieking and dying on the tips of the twin blades. It is a sea of vile monsters against a pair of mere mortals, and the mortals are winning. Some of the demons run, afraid of the power before them, afraid of the light and the strength and the sheer will of their opponents. At last Laurel knows that they fear her. She and Damerin must win.

She rages then, on and on, and this is where Damerin's mercy ends. They are more than they have ever been before. On the thirteenth night, the pair stands together, Laurel and Damerin, perfected. They drive the demons back, floor by floor, into a permanent retreat. They push past the last of the spindly demons to their masters, the great masses of evil whose shrieks are like the bats of hell. One by one, they deal with the great horned, fanged, winged, screaming demons, and they reach the ninth floor.

As they enter the ninth floor, the villagers begin to sing for the last night. The last night before the seventh day of the seventh month that means the end of their hope. Before Laurel and Damerin, in the final level of the keep, resides the one true evil they have been fighting against. It is the shadow that looms over The Palace. It is the dark and powerful creature that has instilled fear into the hearts of every villager for so long. It has no name. It is old and malevolent and churning with rage.

For a long moment, everything in The Palace is still. Then the voices of the villagers singing songs of hope come drifting into the room. Laurel and Damerin, injured and for the first time weary, steel themselves for the last fight.

The shadow looms, waiting for them, eager to obliterate the pests that have entered its domain and refused to die like the rest. It is fighting for its very existence, for all of the power that it has won and lost over the years. It is fighting for the fear and terror it has instilled into the hearts of the people. It is fighting for itself and for all of evil.

They are fighting for the villagers—for the frightened, for the lost, for the weary. They are fighting for each other— for hope, for love, for all things good and right. They are fighting for their pasts and their futures, for the way things should have been and could have been if not for the shadow that has consumed The Palace.

In the same instant that the shadow attacks, Laurel and Damerin do the same. They raise their swords against the shadow, but this is more than a sword fight. This is a battle of souls. The shadow is smothering and great, and the force of its fury is like a tidal wave. But together, the mortals are stronger than ever. Their swords and their souls match the shadow for its every move. For every wound it deals out, it receives a match.

It goes on and on, a cycle within a cycle. The battle rages until the villagers stop singing, until dawn breaks, and until the sun begins to set again. The warriors do not notice. They know only the fight before them. The next block, the next cut, the force of their own wills battle against the shadow's. Eternal. Unbroken.

That is when it happens.

The Palace

13

All parties are injured, tired, fighting with the last of their strength. The two mortals against an evil older than time itself.

Damerin stumbles. Laurel watches in horror as the shadow latches onto him. It drags at him, rips its claws into his armor and tears it away like paper. She screams in anguish and anger as the only person she has ever loved is destroyed in front of her. She can do nothing.

She watches as his light is extinguished. She sees the last message in his eyes. The one thing he never said, but that she always knew. *You are my angel*, his eyes say. *I love you.* Then he is gone, consumed by the darkness before her. Obliterated. She is alone.

Alone and in the dark. But she can see. Suddenly, she understands everything—why he was light, and she was dark. Why she changed, and he did not. It was for this moment. So that she can see and fly and sense the evil all around her. So that she can change.

Her grief, her sorrow, her anger well inside of her like the eye of a divine hurricane. She feels it build and build until it erupts in a scream as she leaps towards the darkness. From her body, true magic explodes outward with all the violence of the storm she has always been. It radiates from her fingertips, her eyes, her sword, and even her scream itself. A great wall of fiery thorns plunges into the shadow, the evil, tearing at it. Burning, burning as dark and hot as Laurel and as bright and pure as Damerin. And so the shadow dies.

14

On the seventh day of the seventh month, the shadow leaves the palace. The spell is broken. The villagers walking in their parade of candles arrive to the palace in all of its old glory.

The gates are open. The turrets and buttresses shine in the light. As they approach, they hear a woman singing.

It is evening, and her voice sounds like light. They find her in the tallest keep in the center of the castle, holding the body of the only man she ever loved, mourning him. They know her.

And so Laurel becomes the Queen of Legend and Damerin her king. And the village never forgets.

The Palace

About The Author

Sophie Rathmann is a young author currently attending Brandeis University. Her passions are centered around English, education, art, and horseback riding. She enjoys all forms of nerd culture and has a love affair with food of all kinds.

About The Publisher

Story Shares is a nonprofit focused on supporting the millions of teens and adults who struggle with reading by creating a new shelf in the library specifically for them. The ever-growing collection features content that is compelling and culturally relevant for teens and adults, yet still readable at a range of lower reading levels.

Story Shares generates content by engaging deeply with writers, bringing together a community to create this new kind of book. With more intriguing and approachable stories to choose from, the teens and adults who have fallen behind are improving their skills and beginning to discover the joy of reading. For more information, visit storyshares.org.

Easy to Read. Hard to Put Down.

CPSIA information can be obtained
at www.ICGtesting.com
Printed in the USA
BVHW052253060223
657976BV00027B/341